William Batchelder Greene

Cloudrifts at Twilight

William Batchelder Greene

Cloudrifts at Twilight

ISBN/EAN: 9783337269456

Printed in Europe, USA, Canada, Australia, Japan

Cover: Foto ©Andreas Hilbeck / pixelio.de

More available books at **www.hansebooks.com**

CLOUDRIFTS AT TWILIGHT

BY

WILLIAM BATCHELDER GREENE

AUTHOR OF "REFLECTIONS AND MODERN MAXIMS"

———

NEW YORK AND LONDON

G. P. PUTNAM'S SONS

The Knickerbocker Press

1888

Press of
G. P. Putnam's Sons
New York

CONTENTS.

iii

CONTENTS.

PROEM.

Endowered bliss of Earth's rejoicing tide,
Whose red gold light alone is poesie,
Whose tinted coming buries deep the snows,
Whose gay horizon promises thy kiss
On every frozen cheek turned heavenward—
Thou Queen incessant of God's harmony !

Reviving Spring, a toast to thy fresh lips !
Thy blush is music, and e'en heaven lurks
In thy thick perfumed hair that hangs about
Thy flowered shoulders like enchanted rain ;
Thy sigh is song and thy soft breath a balm,
Dispelling death—soft loosing his cold grip,
Unravelling darkness in the heart of pain,
As o'er dank waters rings the laugh of dawn.
In thy glad eyes the sun should never set,
For the stars' sake, since they are dumb to men.
Why should man sin or woman sinless fall
When thou dost yearly weep in bliss o'er both,
Decked in deep velvet of God's vernal pomp ?

LARYAT.

SUGGESTED BY THE LEGEND OF TANNHÄUSER.

LARYAT.

Land of perennial Spring,
Blest haven's dells
Whose Easter bells
O'er placid waters ring,
O sea-chained Isle !
Green anchored plot
Of rose-lipped smile—
Soft sea-nymph's kiss—
Sweet dimple—epitome of Paradise
Art thou : foam-nestling nest of Thaura !
Whose feet the feathery sea-down laves,
Whose hands are spray in bloom of Flora—
Oasis 'mid the nodding waves—
O pearl in emerald without price !

Soft fly the zephyrs to thy bosom's shade
To sip of frail-cupped roses perfume laid ;
With the same breath, the birds above
From out the blue,
Of rainbow hue,
Come too—with hymnlettes of their love.
While from a flor-cowled grotto sunk to
    sight,
Inclining low to God's commands
The gray priest raises quivering hands,
Praying that Sacred Love may ne'er take
    flight—
And that it be the bid of fate
That Princess Estha rule the State.

" Princess Estha and her train,
Rulers of Thaura and the main."

The King had not been shrouded long,
Yet was his image stamped in song

Of lyric breath.

Outliving death

Was Estha, with the King's eyes pure :

Resounding, Thaura's hills acclaim

The daughter in the father's name.—

And dew-eyed mounts she to the ivory
   throne,

While all the Bards kneel prone to greet—

To kiss her snowy, trembling feet ;

Entwining music's airy light, if lone

Of soul, about her angel heart—

Invoking heaven by their art

Before the noble throng

In tier, on tiers, along

The echoing walls

Of the deep halls.

As when released, grief's emblems blossom
   white,

So lit each brow ; high voices rang
And drenched the lyres as they sang,
How from mute night spring joys of
    halycon light,
And o'er the pyre drops the screen :—
Their dead King lived in their young
    Queen !
The moon's shade whispered out the news
As silver surf caressed the shore
Before a gold-prowed bucentaur
Whose crew were poets, and the muse
Breathed on their lyres as they passed ;
And roused the vast
Sea-cradled night
Where the barred moonbeams smote with
    light
Between the broken shafts of cloud,
Their pæans loud !

Glad, yet spirit veiled with tear-kissed
    eyes,
The Queen deserting her bright throne
Stops, and slowly smiling, softly sighs,—
She walked alone :
" He 's passing beauteous," she thought.
And as she paused beneath a lattice old
That oped to heaven's arch, Diana caught
Her hair and spun a wreath of gold ;
And shadows whispered : " Sweet and
    pure
Is gold-crowned Estha, chaste of wing !"
And voiceless echoes spake demure :
" Of him that 's beauteous we 'll sing !"
And Estha once more sighed,
Yet no more mourned nor wept ;
And Phœbus rose wide-eyed
Before Diana slept.

Of deeds in words not new to us
We 'll sing of him that 's beauteous ;
Of him who conjured the Queen's smile,
Whose song was sweeter than the rest,
Whose feats were glories of the Isle,
Whose walks were open and were blest :
Laryat his name.
One of Thaura's minstrel band,
Fair rang his fame
Throughout the wave-locked land.
Beyond, he 'd never ventured yet ;
Still, when the fisher cast his net,
His eye would wander outward o'er
The far prone water line,
As if to scan some orient shore
Loosed from the sea's confine.
Not wearied out of exploits in his
    strength—

His strength too keen to rest—

The tide-lulled days had waxed of life-
reft length ;

And seldom seemed night blest

Save when on emerald tiptoe mounts the
moon—

Or his far-sight was fixed at dream-land's
noon ;

Yet even then must come the rousing
sore,—

For 't was at best but a self-phantomed
shore

He rather felt, than saw : to shine no
more—

But ruthless fade away

When smote the hurtling day.

'T was thus, when night's great rafters
break,

He loathed the seeming trespass of the
    dawn,
And almost with despair beheld the morn
With rosy light of dream-robbed garlands
    wake ;
Less fair than sunless, seemed to him
Bright Nature's cup filled to the brim
With teeming waters blest,
Distilled from painless rest.
Half envious scans he now the marble keep,
Where bright a hundred lyres start from
    sleep
With dulcet ringing come again—
Whose measured throb, like silv'ry rain
Falls free on heaven as on lea—
That rippling runs along the sea,
Awaking wave and wastrel sprite
With twinkling throbs of sound and light.

When Laryat raised his dew-stained harp,
And on the damp threads pressed :
It twanged a screech—dissonant sharp,—
Discordant with the rest.

" My Queen, my Queen ! " he helpless
    cried,
As up he sprang,—caught her still face
    apart ;
Their eyes met, and she soft replied :
" It cannot be my Song Bird 's lost his
    art ? "

" Fair Queen, thy Song Bird is undone !
His strength and art droop with the day ;
He 'd tasted heaven, e'er he 'd heaven
    won—
From heaven now must fly away !
Thy servant 's seen a beck'ning ray
Deep in the night—brighter than day !

Away—away! 'T was red-mouthed, mad
    desire
That peeped through curtained welkin,—
    dart of fire !
Mayhap it prove a treasure land,
Must venture there to test its sweet,
Returning thence at thy command
To pour its bounties at thy feet."

" I love not star-gems nor red gold,"
Sighed Estha, and her heart ached cold.

" I will bring songs, plucked from a strange
    land's breast,
Of flame and sun-thought to thy feast,
With brands and love-sparks from the East
To dazzle thy cold bards ; should but my
    quest

Not too audacious seem—
Too temerous my dream?"

And sadly turned aside the Queen—
As if she had naught heard—nor seen.

Save on the night, this pseudo sun rose
    not ;
Yet, like a flashing jewel to his eyes,
Its rays diverging carmined all his skies,—
And in its sheen young Laryat cast his lot.

That night he slipped out on the tide
And turned his back on Thaura's isle.
His sail had veiled the light awhile,
And silent night was ocean's bride
That held him 'twixt their bosoms prest :
An anxious, but a willing guest.

Then stealing o'er the wave the moon arose,
And through the shrouds played the night-
    wind
As 't were a whisp'ring lyre, whose soft
    flows
Bid farewell to the wake behind.

On crest, o'er crest, mounts the bowed bark,
That part like wings in the blue dark.
The moments speed, the hours glide away ;
Till to Dawn's eyes grows faint the beck'-
    ning ray.

Flung wide the East, and paled Diana
    there,
Before a mountain's vine-clad brow
That, terrible in beauty, pierced the air
From out the swaying surf below.

Now 'bout the bark strange water-beings
    sport,
That striped as rainbows dive and flare,
Of wing-like fins and azure streaming hair.
And not far distant Laryat 'spied his port;
A water-grove, with huge pied-grapes o'er-
    hung,
Whose red juice dropped into the brine,
Upon the breasts of mermaids as they
    sung,
And with their white arms shook the vine.

SONG OF THE NAIADS.

How welcome the stranger!
We 'll welcome his suit—
The strong-limbed sea-ranger—
With pipe and with lute;

List soft to his coming,
   Shells, rosy, wide-eared ;
Sing, winds, that are humming,
   And kiss his salt beard !
Come flock now below him,
   And muse in his face ;
For, seeing, we know him
   And willing embrace.
O come, then, light-hearted
   To jest by his side ;
With breasts that are parted,
   We 'll each be his bride !

So blithe and 'witching were their voices
   raised,
That Laryat paused and half turned pale,
As almost unawares the bark's keel grazed
The low lip of the land-mouth's rail.

Then weird-eyed shells so smote his eyes,

That he stood wav'ring, dazed, irresolute,

While from the heights came such soft
sighs,

As erewhile all sweet love-notes had
seemed mute.

Then saw he glancing silv'ry feet across

The shells, as white and light as snow or
moss.

He raised his head : a thousand damsels
shone

With that soft sheen that flashes from fair
limbs ;

Their girdles knit of flower's eyes, and on

Their heads they held gold cups with
dripping brims ;

While by the flowers that she wore :

By Jessamine, by Rose or Violet,

By Daisy, Snow-drop, Lilly, Tulip met—
Each called the other on the shore.

SONG OF THE HANDMAIDS OF THE VINE.

We are the handmaids of the Vine,
    More beautiful than she;
Yet not so powerful to twine,
    And loose man's spirits free.
Come drink! before ye enter in;
And think—O think not Love a sin!
While these beguile the air with jest and
    smile,
Child Laryat lightly leaves his bark ere-
    while,
Sips but a drop from each cupped flower's
    head,
And up the mountain's vine-webbed spur
    is led,

Where droops the luscious, swollen, hoar-
    flushed grapes,

And myrrh-like incense from flag-root es-
    capes.

Then sprite-like beings 'mid the vines ap-
    pear ;

The coy yet tameless Satyr lends his ear,

As the loosed huntsman's hound

That starts at every sound.

And as trunk-woven vistas opened out

In semi sun-barred far diverging rays,

Young Laryat heard a strange wild
    echoed shout,

And saw athletic girls that danced, as fays

And imps might sport beneath a moon-
    cloud's rift ;

Of sun-kissed skin and without girth or
    shift.

SONG OF THE DRYADS.

Aha! men think us rough and rude,
　For we are strong and bold and free;
We are the forest's simple brood,
　The Servants of Love's fairy dell,
Slaves of our Queen, whose girdle is
　　　Rare Asphodel.

Aha! Aha! Our panting Queen—
　Lithe as a serpent in her bed;
She writhes with mad throes on the
　　green,
　She leaves her kisses where they fell—
As half unloosed is her bright wreath
　　　Of Asphodel.

Aha! Aha! The lusty sport—
　The Satyr big and strong of haunch,

With buck and gambol and hoarse snort,
  We make him hot and prick'ling well
For our Queen, whose girdle is
    Choice Asphodel.

Then came a crash! The Satyrs in one
   throng
Swept with wild snorts the shrieking
   girls along.

SONG OF THE SATYRS.

   Shrews
     Of the horn!
   Spawn
     Of the mews!

" These are not meet," quoth one—
His hands upon his hirsute knees,

To Laryat pausing 'neath the trees,—
" For him shaped in the full mould of a
    god !
Fear'st thou to meet the Sun ?
Seek higher for a fitter love
By the Empyrean's Myrtle Grove ;
Leave the grapes' shade,—its bouts and
    wine-stained sod."

SONG OF THE HANDMAIDS OF THE VINE.

Higher
    Above
Aspire
    To love.

With mutterings,
Weird utterings,

Fawn-lisps, stray gestures blent—scarce
    understood :
Sir Laryat reached the flare kirt' of the
    wood.
A tarn was there, nursed by a crystal
    stream,
Like a round crater, dead and black.
Laryat advanced as in a waking dream—
But quick, the damsels drew him back :
'T was the dark Mirror of the Fauns
That gives to man the hoofs and horns !

Then soared to skies a hymn of praise,
Whose strident chords fell on the now
    dumb wold ;
While there were angels coming to his
    'maze,
Not white of robe—but of red-tinted fold.

SONG OF THE RETAINERS OF EROS.

We are the Disciples of Flame,
Of Cupid and joys without name;
We dwell in the depths of man's heart,
Concealed in its yearnings apart,
Where patient we wait Cupid's art
To welcome the smart of his dart.
The Soul is a beautiful shrine
That burns at Love's whispers divine;
That trembles in tumult of bliss—
Returning red-passion's long kiss.

Athwart the sun's eyes rose the seraph's
    wings.
From that time on, all sung and moved
    in trance;
A thought of Thaura came and went;
    a glance

As 't were at Estha, and at dreamlike
    things ;
The present and the pageant seemed all
    real,
'T was but the past he could no longer feel.
The future promised was love's dazzling
    shore—
The present sweet : what recked Child
    Laryat more ?

To the grove of myrtles that blow
O'er ravished rust-shackles of care—
Where cleft is the knit-brow of woe ;
O waft wind away to that sea—
Fleet cloud of full-bosomed winged air,
Where Venus sprang flashing and free !
To the wave, the foam-nestling shell,
The grotto of tinsel and jet,

To ocean's unfathomed green well
Where Love-dawn first flung out his net!
Where rocked in the caves of his birth,
Naught knowing of sorrows on earth ;
Self-drowned in locked bliss for a night,
Upheaving the main with his might,
Whose torrents the darkness obeyed :
Love broke forth to Man—as a Maid !

There was a fragrance that the heights
    imbued—
That he then felt, not seeing—
That thrilled through all his being ;
As still they sped in dazzling altitude.—
Was it a phantom from the grapes?
He fancied that each sphere-like cloud
Was fraught with twin-embracing shapes,
The music swelling still more loud.

Neared he the blithe, ecstatic shore ? . . .
His head sank—and he recked no more.

With sight unsealed, 't was as to bliss he
'woke :
To transport as of trance, joy unbereaved ;
While o'er his beard there thrilled an
am'rous stroke,
And by his cheek a throbbing bosom
heaved.
And when he looked, he gazed into two
eyes
More deep, more blue, than Orient's un-
veiled skies !
So still, they seemed to gaze beyond on
space ;
So bright their waters, he scarce saw the
face.

"What angel holds me now in fond embrace?"

"No angel am I, but thy love,
Born in the Myrtle's sacred Grove.—
I' ve tarried for thee, Laryat, Time's spent
space."

"Thou art perfection's mould, and still
more fair!
Thy breasts, thy lips—thy 'witching, silk-
seine hair."

"All that is mine is thine
If but thy thought be mine?"
Marking her smile and nod—he opes his
arms—
Burning he stoops and intent clasps her
charms.

Pleased with her capture—
    Complacent her smile;
Conscious in rapture
    Of weaving her wile;
Abandoned to one
    Whose passion is true,
Longs for another
    That 's dif'rent and new.

Lithe in caresses,
    The pink of her sex,
Loose are her tresses
    Her leman to vex;
Vine-like her graces
    Far-look in her eyes,
Firm her embraces
    And trembling her sighs.

Dawn, thou art breaking
    And night, thou art spent,

Dream-bliss forsaking,
Thy curtain is rent ;
Flown is Love's token !
His power is gone :
Cupid, heart-broken,
Lies sobbing alone !

Hast thou not sauntered in love's per-
fumed halls ;
Their pavement knit of twining maids,
Of smooth, white limbs and knotted
braids ;
Hast marked the starry mirrors on the
walls,
Reflecting moon-sheen on the musk-
dewed beds
Of tiger-lilies with flushed drooping heads ?
Hast not been drunk with incense 'neath
the bine ;

Hast thou not pressed the lilac, lashed
    with vine;
Hast thou not known the Goddess crown
    the shrine :
Her bosom's pearl-blush, and her veil—
Revealing flashes of blithe undreamt
    bliss—
Woven of Virgins' tears, too frail
To bear e'en the soft breath of leman's
    kiss?

Passions of night 'wake anguish by day;
Temples that burn, to ashes decay.

And on the red Mount, Laryat lingered
    long,
Beguiled by thrallen love—by wine and
    song.
Till waxed and waned his lordly mood,

Until he loathed the scalding food
Of which his chilled blood now seemed
　　satiate,
And longed to fly, e'er Fate might bar the
　　gate.
To turn from facile conquests now grown
　　vain,
His wak'ning Soul was rife ;
To taste and feel the freedom once again
Of unenchanted life.

"And thou wouldst leave me reft for
　　years !"
Sighed his Enchantress 'neath her tears.

" The days seemed long,—and nights are
　　short."
He made retort.

" Thou hast another love, more dear
In thy thought's eyes—I fear.
Ah ! cruel, soulless is thy sex that cling
Not unto any thing !"

" Fair Dame, thou art as beauteous as the
      Day ;
Yet still, I must away."

" I 've stood above a sun-strewn stream
And   seen   my   svelte   wraith — as   in
      dream
That 's ravishing—gaze mocking there ;
So pure—inviolate and fair ;
Like the twin-semblance of our Queen,
Who sits Perfection Throned, serene.
And still I ponder—puzzled now,
How thou could'st be revolted—thou ! . .

Yet have I solace, since we part;
My image is stamped on thy heart;
So any virgin thou embrace
Shall see my spirit in thy face!
And when thou wed,—then think on me—
For then : the clasped hands shall be
  three!"

"Moon-drunk thou art! And dost thou
  deem I can
Be gudgeoned thus—if still I be a man?
Dost dream I'd quail before such shrewish
  burst?"

" Am I not meet for any god?
If not chastise me with a rod;
Cast my loose flesh to any swine,
That hate sweet waters and love brine;

That must be goaded with a prod
And made to eat when they 're in luck,—
As some daft brutish Satyr buck!
I 've Princes known—in love's brief hour—
Who awed and ravished, lost their power
At the mere magic of my rod!
Thou must not linger here, for thou art
　　'cursed;
Nor 'bout our haunted woodlands roam—
Seeking, forsooth, a better home!
Yet spare me this low leering bow.
Yea—I am glad th' 'rt going now!
Take—drink this cup of slumber juice,
Fear naught—thou 'lt rid me by its use,—
Yet see that none be spilt—
'T will take thee where thou wilt:
To Heaven or to Hell—
And so: Farewell!"

"Awhile farewell, fair Dame!
To prove to thee, I think
Thou lov'st me still the same :—
See—to the dregs I drink!"
Fixed on far Thaura's quiet skies,
Faint Laryat closed his swooning eyes.

Sweet pipers of advancing dawn
Forgetful the slain night to mourn,
Note-wastrels, choral birds
Whose songs are without words ;
More musical—profoundly true
Than words could well express
The infinite of Heaven's blue
On Earth's bright loveliness ;
Glad gaolers of enveloped strife—
Forerunners with the Torch of Life.
Laryat awoke in Thaura's Isle,
And rushed to kiss the monarch's hand.

Estha embraced him with a smile,
And gave rejoicings through the land;
In every ear his journey's fame—
On every lip his name.

The heralds sounded with trumpet to court
The young Queen passed with her train;
Close to the poets, who sat wrapt in
    thought,
The trumpets sounded again;
Then forth Child Laryat stood
Like a tall young tree
That shakes his branches free,
From out the low'ring wood.

The monarch's still voice rose: "Yet once
    again
We give bard Laryat welcome to this
    Realm,

Glad that bereavement's sail hath shift to
    gain ;
Since, like an able steersman at his helm
Conspiring with Love's tides, returning
    he
Brings safe to port his song's gold ar-
    gosy."
Then comes the pause of an expectant
    hush—
And Laryat's fingers o'er the bright cords
    rush.

O Queen of the Isle and the main—
    And sun of my sail-wingèd car !
      I 'd fling to the sea this fell lute
If aught that it spake should seem vain—
    Unworthy of Estha's chaste star ;
      'T were better my lips stricken mute !

Then listen, O Queen, to tne rhyme
  Of one who hath supped of mad bliss
    In a land where Love is born free ;
Where breast unto bosom doth chime
  To the rhyme in the soul of one kiss
    That is heaven ! over the sea.

A mount where the night 's ever bright
  With the Light of passion's wild flame
    And the flash of Cupid's red bow
O'er its crest that with fair limbs is white !
  To which Love-feasts of Thaura were
    tame,
    Though the main with wine should
    o'erflow.

Like the hoarse breathings of a sourdent
  gale

Low muttered murmurs ran—the Queen
  was pale.

O that ye would list to my song,
  That ye all might learn what is Love—
   And knowing, in Love's Goddess be-
    lieve !
Ye courtiers and bards in the throng
  That look not on earth, but above,
   For blessings ye never receive !

At this—the clamor brake,
As of old Babel burst from night anew.
Then rose—as madder still the tumult
  grew—
A hoary bard, who had not sung for years,
And fixed the Queen—who sought to
  screen her tears—
And thus the old man spake :—

" Conceive perfected marble with the
breath
Of Being, without Death.—
Embodied in such bodies in the Flame,
The Serpent's touch, that burns without a
name,
Achieve the acme of the Passion's sense :
And where Love ends, commence
Around the panting zones that flash
White-hot, and drop chaste Love as art ;
Believe in this mad heaven of unrest ;—
Or fly—and be ye blest ! "

Then smote he Laryat's lyre from his
hand !
While Laryat gasping—losing self-com-
mand—
Quick grasped his sword-hilt with a fren-
zied glare,

While 'bout him flashed full fifty blades
　　in air :
" Thou Turk !　Would'st strike a frail old
　　man ?" cried one.
"Of thee, and thy vile songs we will have
　　none !"
Then 'twixt the combatants pale Estha
　　stood
Alone, at first in calm, collected mood :—
" Sirs, ye forget yourselves—the place—
My presence here, 't would seem ! . . .
Yet if this be a dream—
'T is shameful !" and she hid her face,
Anguish in her sobs revealed.—
Laryat brake his sword—and kneeled.

RES JUDICATA.

When leaves are pressed against the hot
bent sky
Night giving in their shade ; their cool
webbed hands
Thrust out the ardent sun as should chaste
maid's,
As green-haired wavelets scolloped on
the shore
Of the unfrozen blue that burns o'er-
head ;
When alien waters meet in headlong feud
Awhile they strive with spray uplifted
wings
Then pause—embrace in flowery beds of
foam

And sink into a double depth more tranquil

Then the first that gave them single birth ;

And so cloud-bred conflicting winds, con-
flict

No more once met, but wed their breaths
in calm ;

So flame to flame is fire met.   But our

Days are ground out in unrestfulness,

While night-tides tread upon their skirts
with balm

Made precious only by the strife of light;

The beast is tamed and Heaven's promised
Man.

'T is given us to weigh by touch—to con

The hornèd Evil and the far-wing'd Good,

Yet neither Spirit in World-wounded
breasts

Can give Man peace : *because the other is.*

TENEBRÆ.

SELF.

Yet comes my mood again,

But with a greater pain.

In all the world, most in the world, alone!

Like some deserted monarch on his
throne—

Oppressive stillness closes me around,

As if to shut out hope without a sound.

How tomb-like seems this haunt in dreary
plight—

Meet vault for death! And where the
bilious light

Falls on the walls, I hideous Shadows
see—

Like ghouls, that grin and nod, in hellish
  glee!

THE SHADOWS ON THE WALLS.

Stand still
The Will?
Arrant madness,
Born of sadness
Seeks only for repose.
The strife
Of life?
Going, sowing-
Never knowing
'T is flowing to its close.
The breath
Of death?
Bosom aching
Nature quacking
But Self-damnation knows!

SELF.

Dread terror now doth shroud me in the
    very air!
While cold, insidious—the monster Grim
    Despair
Doth sink into my soul this last appeal:
How with 'cursed Life it were now best
    to deal!
Th' oppressive walls about me seek to meet
E'en strong floor uplifts beneath my feet!
As if to press and hasten on the end—
Ere I repent or Angels should defend!
My senses reel! Quick, let me yield to
    fate!
Where is the vial, ere it be too late!

The hand of Dawn is in the East.
    Sweet stars! on tip-toe in the trem'bling
      sky;

Oh, take me with you to the feast
 Whereto ye go! Ye cannot shake me.
  Why?
I can no longer rest below,
 Earth's bars imprison me by night and
  day!
Were I a spirit—might I go?
 But stay—I 'll drain this cup, and then
  away!
We 'll go together to those Lands
 Where dwell—beyond the pale of mor-
  tal sight—
Those weary ones, with folded hands:
 Whose wings unfurled, outstretched,
  and sought the Light!

A VOICE FROM ABOVE.

"Ye are bought with a price!" *

* I. Corinthians, Chapter vi., verse 20.

PARNASSUS.

True poetry is not of earth,
'T is more of Heaven by its birth;
A mingled feeling keeps us tied
Fast down to earth where we abide;
Close to the precipice of Time
We eager creep with ventured rhyme,
There stunned and staggered to behold
The wonders of great truths untold,
And fearful lest we lose our hold,
Or mute—dumbfounded at the sight—
The Muse recedes, or checks her flight.

Truth—truth! 't is all a poet's cry;
But earth comes in to give the lie ·

E'en man's best nature is impure,
And cannot too much light endure;
We 're happy still, content at least
With what crumbs fall from Nature's feast;
'T is like a glass—truth but reflects,
Though darkly, through our intellects,
Clouded by care, or scarce aware
What great things God would picture
    there.

AMERICANUS.

'T is the custom of our Country, and a
    greater there is none,
That all callings, trades, or business, you
    may now combine in one.
Man's vocations each I 've filled, from the
    greatest to the least,
Like a Buddhist that has sojourned 'neath
    the pelt of every beast ;
I have been a Gospel preacher, a general
    and commodore,
I 'm a thing of stock exchanges and a doc-
    tor of the law.
Of the book of my professions I 've heeded
    not the text—

If you fail an undertaking, it 's so easy to
    say " next."
" Next!" I 've cried, " I 'll try another,"
    until wearisome it grew—
Pretending to be knowing, when I really
    nothing knew.
Puritans my fathers were—and they have
    had their day;
And " gorgeousness " I crave not—in the
    bourgeois sort of way.
" Nobodies" I cannot envy, who from out
    the gutter rise,
Parading vulgar millions, here before
    men's hungry eyes.
Riches make the cad more churlish.   Need
    or want man's patience tries—
Crushing out what hope is in him, when-
    soe'er he seeks to rise.

Air, light! Give me Freedom, I don't
    want the empty name,
I don't want the hollow carcass, whence
    hath fled fair honor's flame;
To the highest give him power, to the low-
    est give him bread,
To the demagogue and bully listen not in
    silent dread;
Be a Man! and God will rescue this Great
    Country from their hand—
Keep thy "Birth-right" as the jewel to
    illumine all the Land!

"NOT YET SIXTEEN."

A LETTER.

" Dear Husband Fred :.
    Come to your little wife ;
  I ought to love you and I dŏ—
  I did not mean to worry you ;
I won't toss ball with Mary any more.
  I quite agree with all you say,
  A married girl should never play.

" And Fred, I won't regret that I 've left
    school ;
  But only I do feel so old,
  And all the girls say I 'm so cold
And stiff, because I wear a cap and train.
  But married ladies must dress so,
  As they 're quite old enough to know.

56

" The house seems—oh ! so big and still,
    dear Fred,
When you are gone. And when Nurse,
    too,
Is cross, I don't know what to do !
I can't skip rope ; it makes the servants
    laugh—
I heard them whisper on the green :
' Poor Mis'ess ! She 's not yet sixteen.'

' I 'll let them know what I 'm about ;
I 've made a nest up in a tree,
Where there's just room for you and me;
And when those *children* come, I 'll say
    I 'm *out*,—
I 'll show them what is married life !
Won't that be right ?
            " Your little wife."

AN INVOCATION.

Thou Moon! Sun of the Night,
  Sister mystic of the Day;
Look down, pause in thy flight!
  Calm me with thy aural ray,
Enchanting souls to silver sleep.
Look down from out thy airy keep,
My fevered senses hypnotize;
Shut out the World, whereto Mind flies—
Ambitious Mind, with travail sore;
Its fibre rest, its calm restore.

CELESTIAL ANSWER.

Above the care of Nature and of State,
Suspended in the noon of Night we wait,

All slumber nursing, to make sweet and
pure,
While secret Nature, weaving works the
cure.
We are the handmaids of the hollow
night,
The angels of the dark, restoring sight ;
We go—the pains of Day to soothe, con-
sole—
Awake, arise ! Behold thou art made
whole.

KNOWLEDGE IS NOTHING;
ELSE MAN COULD CREATE.

Behold my labors' lumbered battle-ground;

These volumes, charts, like dead men
strewn around,

Whose leaves I 've dog-eared—till I could
no more—

With patience delving to exhume the lore

From Zoroaster unto Faraday,

The lesser profit gleaming on the way;

For more I 've done! I 've studied Odic
Force;

And can arrest a spirit in its course;

I know Man's aura well, and all its freaks,

And read my neighbor's thoughts before
he speaks;

The vital force of Life I can distil,

Yea, more ! for now, at last, I 've mastered
   Vril.*

But to what purpose !   I 'm but flesh and
   blood.

All things are vain—and knowledge but a
   flood

Submerging all my better self—my heart,

And doth to Man but callousness impart.

Still I am chained—still but a stifled
   wretch—

Within the human bonds of "go and
   fetch " ;

And like some stale—some dingy, old professor,

I am a prey to spleen, and qualms, and
   error.

---

* See Bulwer's " Coming Race."

*Knowledge is nothing ; else man could Cre-
      ate !*

Drowned in " Equality," this is Man's
      state—

A ripple on vast " Freedom's " ocean
      tossed,

His Individuality is lost !

I 'm like a number in a numbered street,

E'en to be hated—even that were sweet !

As for success ! Quacks need but *say*
      they 're great

To snatch what laurels *we 'd* anticipate.

MISERABILE DICTU!

Whatever this may be,
   'T is e'en for the best;
Though a shudder comes o'er me,
   Thy soul is at rest.

In the Church-Yard alone,
   Sweet child, thou art sleeping;
While the billows do moan,
   And the heavens are weeping.

Since men have forbidden—
   My darling, 't is better for thee,
That the Grave hath all hidden,
   And thy father should flee;

Yet thy spirit is near,
 On the wings of the gale—
Yea, darling, thou 'rt here,
 By my storm-beaten sail.

I hear thy voice calling ;
 'T is sweetly the same,
O'er the tempest appalling,
 That is calling my name.

In fondness I follow,
 Though swift be thy flight,
In the silence of sorrow
 And the darkness of night !

THE MESHES.

Behold! loud pageant and strained heart
With chiselled gilt encasing soulless rags ;
A nerveless hand that clings to quivering
    mesh
Out-spun by a faint mirage of loose hopes
From the hot caldron of far speeding aims,
A flickering dream to dance in fire-light—
Consumed to life in flame—to ashen life ;
A breath may kindle, while yet not a
    flood—
Misfortune's rack—can wholly chill the
    pulse
That 's fever-lashed for future's looming
    bourns ;

So dry in thirst that sees an empty cup !

Not till the rose is torn are thorns with
blood,

And life's long covetings die crownless
bliss—

Or sigh-sick forms turn vapors packed
with wraiths ;

Stops dead day's dial if our hopes feign
night—

The present dying bids the future pause ;

Till wisdom come, man's heart goes up no
more.

THE TOAST TO NEW ENGLAND.

Fill up the bowl and let us sing;
Loud let our gladsome voices ring
O'er land and sea, where'er men roam :
A greeting to our brave old Home,
      New England !

She beat the French, She beat the Dutch,
And yet we count this not so much;
But stiff and strong the old brew mix,
And let us drink to " 76,"
      New England !

Then came that trouble on the sea,
Where both sides fought so gallantly :

What put the spokes in John Bull's game?
The simple magic of that Name,
   New England!

Last came that strife where Brothers met,
And Mothers' hearts are bleeding yet;
For years we fought like desp'rate men:
What saved the Union, there and then?
   New England!

Yet once again in parting raise
Unto our lips the cup of praise;
We drink: *Long Life!* to Thee and
  Thine—
My proudest boast to call Thee mine,
   New England!

THE LINK.

Some fearful sights there be that creep
By night—I mean that harass sleep ;
But tenfold more alarming seem these
    when
They brave the day, to breathe the air
    like men ;
With us—like us, of life partaking ;
From *such*, alas ! there 's no awaking,
Some dark presentiment their aura bears—
I know not what ?—of something un-
    awares ;
As when in dreams, our foothold seems
    to miss
And we slip down some deep unknown
    abyss.

THE BALLAD OF LAMENTA-
TIONS.

An old Soul's sorrow—none so gray
By dun of night or flare of day—
     What shall I do ?
The idle, idle fondled dream
Of bliss—burst bubble on the stream !
     What shall I do ?
And looking back, I can count now
The failures that have scarred my brow.
     What shall I do ?
I 'm scarred within—I 'm scarred without ;
     What shall I do ?
The sin of years hath found me out,
     What shall I do ?

God grant th' oblivion I seek !
>   What shall I do ?
God's love was true—t 'was *self* was
>   weak—
>   What shall I do ?
Curse a life's *error ?*   'T is past late.
>   What shall I do ?
All must shift right or left with fate,
>   What shall I do ?
" Forgive thy life "—forget mad trance
That youth thy being could enhance !
>   What shall I do ?

I am alone now that I 'm weak ;
>   What shall I do ?
The echoes whisper when I speak,
>   What shall I do ?
My eyes are as the melting snow—

Time-watered blood as tears that flow.
    What shall I do?
My hand is like the Autumn leaf,
    What shall I do?
Despair steals o'er me as a thief,
    What shall I do?
Though yet afraid, I fain would go.
    What shall I do?
Bent now the bones that raise the form
Unsheathed—still facing every storm!—
    What shall I do?
I'm but a remnant of the past—
Forgotten—beached on present's vast;
    What shall I do?
Repudiated by the night
That snatched my dear ones from my
   sight,
    What shall I do?

Strayed—unfamiliar—lost by day—
 What shall I do ?
Faint stranger that has missed the way ;
 What shall I do ?
That with shrunk sight peers out on space
To greet no one familiar face,
 What shall I do ?
Alone I 'm old—all else is new ;
Save the warm sun, the stars, the blue—
Friends of my youth—the only few,
 What shall I do ?
Dazed at my smile, bright cheeks are pale ;
 What shall I do ?
When beauty turns—draws close her veil,
 What shall I do ?
Had I enough strength left for rage
I 'd snap the white bars of this cage !
 What shall I do ?

I could love well, I could be bold,
    What shall I do ?
Had not love's treasures grown so cold,
    What shall I do ?
Numb icicles close fast love's heart—
Dumb-blighting love, beyond love's art !
    What shall I do ?
My being stark 'wakes with the day,
    What shall I do ?
My soul hath quarrelled with its clay,
    What shall I do ?
Let friendship fill this hollow breast—
Full friendship that heaps balm of rest.
    What shall I do ?
Where   sped—friend   of   the   friendly
    band ?
Gone on for aye—the Promised Land—
    What shall I do ?

Thy flight was swift—fain would I weep!
>What shall I do?
Better than earth—by thee I 'd sleep. . . .
>What shall I do?
Strong men are treading down the earth,
>What shall I do?
The earth that buries and gives birth,
>What shall I do?
Whose blossoms blend both black and
white,
As cycles turning day and night :
>What shall I do?
Sleep smites full years, feigns play with
youth ;
>What shall I do?
To be, and act—yet kneel to truth
Seen as faint star out earth's broad well,
>What shall I do?

As God's hand smites the startled bell;
From anguish unto peace that knell,
> What shall I do?
Great God, I 'll kiss Thy chast'ning rod!
Hark!—Clinks the spade on grassy sod—
> What shall I do?—
Earth's scales have fallen from my sight—
O God, what rapture! O what Light!
> No more to do!

THE NEW PONS ASINORUM.

A CIRCLE WITH A DOT AT THE CENTRE.

This is the test of Man's depravity,
A symbol of the greatest gravity.
Then list, while I try to expound the thing :
The dot is Man, Temptation is the ring.
Say thou 'rt the *dot*—the circle whirls
    around thee,
Becoming narrower—as to confound thee ;
If it come so close that it gulf the *dot*—
Then thou art lost ! Thy life 's a blur—a
    blot.

THE

NEW PROLOGUE IN HEAVEN

TO

AN AMERICAN FAUST.

1884.

Scene :—*Clouds.*

Akem Manô discovered looking down.

AKEM MANÔ.*

To have no youth, no prime, nor age,
  Of Time and Limit thus bereft,
No date, or all, on History's page ;
  My seal 's upon each Record left.

So fated never to know more
Than what, forsooth, I knew before,

* As Mephistopheles.

With still a thirst insatiate,
Advancement is debarred. Yet wait;
For Power can be won by lies
On Earth,—we 'll try it on the Skies!
Men say each dog must have his day;
I limp along the broad World's way,
Oppressed, o'ershadowed by a Name
Greater than mine that bears the shame.

(*Sounds of celestial music are heard.*)

This marks my goal! Upon the cone of
    night,
Shot up from th' eclipsing Earth,
I 've deftly ridden Here.

(*Heaven opens. Angels and redeemed Spirits mingle ;
ascending and descending, to and from a Higher
Region in the distance.*)

                    The Souls in Light!
Behold! ecstatic second birth.

HEAVENLY CHORUS.

Continually we cry, eternally we sing ;

Forever Thou art God, forever Thou art
King !

The glad Song leaps from Oceans of a
Thousand Worlds,

While giant mountains back the sacred
echo hurls:

Praise unto Thee, Thou art the Lord, the
God of All !

Let Heaven, let the Earth, and all Creation
bow,

Fall down and praise ! The Alpha and
Omega Thou.

Through boundless Space—the Spheres
that whirl beneath Thy feet,

To Constellations from afar proclaim, re-
peat :

Praise unto Thee, Thou art the Lord, the
　　God of all!

AKEM MANÔ.

No stock I 'll take in Heaven's stuff,
　　I 'm here on biz, and must look sharp.
For girls, it is all well enough
　　To smile and sing, and twang the harp.
She 's not so bad—I 'll try a wink;
　　These robes do so the form enhance,
Or so a mortal Here would think;
　　They 'd be in Hell! had I the chance.

(Addressing a passing Spirit.*)

" High Mightiness!"†
Whose ghost art thou?
Whose is that leer, that servile bow,

---

*" The Father of his Country.

† One of the forms of addressing the President of the
United States proposed by Adams.

Whose is that snout, that serpent face?
'T is not of Earth, nor of this Place.

AKEM MANÔ.

Well guessed! from both I 've had the
    sack;
For through a crack, from Here I fell,
And I came down with such a whack
That through Earth's crust I went to
    Hell.
Thou mark'st that I 'm a trifle lame,
That was the Fall—I 'm not to blame.

SPIRIT.

Thou trespassing black Ape of Lies,
Thy presence Here pollutes the Skies!
Thou spawn of toad, unburied worm——

AKEM MANÔ.

Enough — and more! You make one
  squirm;
In Spirit conversation there's a leaven;
Let's be polite, since we're in Heaven.

SPIRIT.

Begone from me, Tormenting Fire!
To hearken thus I 've no desire.

AKEM MANÔ.

Here can'st thou not endure a foe?
  I struggled 'gainst thee to my cost;
Yea, I 'm thine enemy; and so
  Forgive thou must—else Heaven 's lost!
Forget that we e'er met before;
Forgive, on this Eternal Shore.
How 's that! I 'm not much good at
  preaching.

Below we rather lack Church teaching ;
But that is neither here nor there ;
   To bandy words is too absurd.
I 'm not up here to split a hair,
   I 've simply come to bring thee word :—
Things are not always what they seem—
Burst is the bubble of Thy Dream !
Thy System 's on its way to rot ;.
   Thy Country each four years is sold
To demagogues, who care no jot
   So long as they can bleed her cold ;
Enrich themselves with Public gold,
As kings were wont to bag of old.
In monarchs' hearts I 'd found it well
   To be ; and if they had no hearts,
Well, then—I 'd in their paunches dwell,
   Therefrom controlling all their parts.
Now all is changed !   The Nations sing

That " Liberty " 's a funny thing !
Things *are* so queer. I 've ceased to roam,
And made it, over there, my home,—
Perchance, but for a little while,
Yet still the thought provokes a smile.

SPIRIT.

Thou 'rt false again !   But I refrain—
Full soon will'st find thou schem'st in vain ;
For there 's a Banner uncorrupt and new,
A Band full strong, though they be few,
Led by Excelse * in armor clad—
He 'll prove thy match, though but a lad !

AKEM MANÔ.

The others are such wretched game ;
Pop ! goes my gun—they 're all too tame.

* As Faust.

Excelse I 'll have, he must atone!
As this concerns thee, I believe,
'T has been exacted by The Throne,
That first of all I crave thy leave.

SPIRIT.

Excelse !   *That* soul can never die.

AKEM MANÔ.

'T is done !   I see thou bid'st me try ;
Thou never erst wouldst tell a lie !

CHORUS OF ANGELS.

While Light, exulting, slays dread Darkness at a bound,
Let Song from Sky to Sky, o'er each abyss
resound.
Sound trumpet, shawm, and timbrel loud.

Acclaim The Day!

For Seraphim with Cherubim prepare the
way!

(*Heaven is flooded with light ; celestial music is heard
at the approach of the Most High.*)

AKEM MANÔ (*looking up*).

Well now!   Not fool, or eagle, am I thus

To squint up at the Sun, you know ;

I 'd rather Heat than Glare—without this
fuss!

There 's no more fun up Here. I 'll go.

(*Heaven closes.*)

AKEM MANÔ (*solus, waving a pinion*).

By George !——

In our Times, 't is rare one can

Converse with such a perfect gentleman.

(*Vanishes.—Thunder.*)

MOTHER.

Mother! intellect and joy—
Sweet patience of my youth,
Boon of my manhood and my strength—
My joy in pain ; my gentle counsellor.

"HEART OF MY HEART."

Heart of my heart, flesh of my flesh, bone
    of my bone,
I love thee for thyself, and for the chil-
    dren that thou gavest me.
Well thou dost bear with me the burden
    of the life I lead,
Companion of my days.   Could they re-
    semble thee,
Accurséd then should be the race that love
    not their own wives !

THE SONG OF THE BIRDS.

Ye wastrels of the sky—whose twinkling
wings
Unveil the stars beneath the sun's near
glow ;
How ye must tnrob of wondrous whispered
things
Unheard below.

'T would be an Angel's task—the wingéd
throng—
To sing of each and all that fill the skies ;
Yet from the wold and plot I 'll raise my
song—
What in me lies.

The matchless Eagle scorns the lowly
　　branch,
But, perched majestic on a summit rock,
Looks on the sun when roars the avalanche
　　Nor heeds the shock !

At dawn the Swan upon the stream
　　awakes ;
　At evening, too, I saw him with his
　　mate,
And from the hills they seemed like snowy
　　flakes
　　　Lost on the lake.

The Lark straight toward the zenith
　　takes her flight,
　And halting even-poised on twinkling
　　wings,

Like a mere speck suspended in the
 light,
  Her pæan sings.

With quivering stir ·the Peacock's tail
 shakes wide,
 'T is pageant's self—a rainbow 'neath the
 skies ;
So struts the haughty bird, its gorgeous
 pride
  The hundred eyes.

I 've known this bird with dead " eyes" in
 the fan—
 Bleached, blotted out—as of a ghostly
 white ;
But 'round the tips a snowy nimbus ran
  Like northern light.

The Parrot's kin is the dumb Cockatoo :
  Thou hast no greeting, unloquacious
    bird !
And yet thy cousin can well speak for two ;
  He 's ever heard..

Awaiting night to give him back his wits,
  Minerva's Bird is badgered by small
    fowl ;
Vexed, on the ruined tower there he sits,
  The blear old Owl !

The Carrier Pigeons like swift arrows go
  High o'er the banned, beleaguered city's
    gate,
And on their wings are traced in 'prisoned
  woe
    Brief words of Fate.

Still patters rain, the woodland's all asop;
But listen to that bright glad note!
List—hush :
It steals between the drops from that tree
top
Where bathes the Thrush.

The common Sparrow let me not forget,
That tame about our walks familiar flies;
Contented with a crumb—a human pet
In poor men's eyes.

To sad, barred windows come the sweet
birds blest ;
And to the sick—unvisited for long—
How welcome sounds, before they sink to
rest,
A good-night song !

God's music 's light—e'en some sad songs
    breathe light
Unto blind darkness that hath only ears :
As when the Nightingale pours forth by
    night
       Her soul in tears.

Ye Angel birds, whose bones are marrow-
    less,
  With pinions stretched in benisons
    above :
Look down from Heaven's arch—from
    there confess
      As spake the Dove !

THE NIGHT, TO WINGÉD SOULS, IS DAY.

I.—THE SPIRIT'S TRYST.

I have a mind enjoyable,
Companion of my soul,
And all the fancies that it feeds
I cannot paint in words.
I climb the mountain on the mist,
Or sweep deep down a vale ;
Strange frost-work pluck I from the
    moon,
And dew-drops from the stars.
I quickly span the earthly zones,
I reach from Pole to Pole,

And like the winds that veer about—
Take wing to East or West.
I go to where my loved-one dreams,
I peep beneath the night,
And in the void where spirits dwell
I press her soul in flight.

II.—THE SOURCE OF LOVE.

Now on the rocks of Spirit-land
We pause, and soft commune,
By that vast deep—Eternity,
Unvisited by Earth.
And at our feet a thousand worlds
Whirr in their curving course;
And, bending low, we catch the sound—
" The music of the stars."
'Round, 'round they go in cadence marked,
Each peopled as of old;

And 'round 'bout each, like parasites,
Wee moons—in shadow bright.
How now!   A comet thunders through,
We kneel and gaze above—
Then veil our eyes, yet weep for joy,—
Behold, it is the Star of Love!
O Paradise! that glorious star!
Speak—stranger, reading this—
Perchance thou 'st felt the rays of Love,
Yet never seen the Source?
    E'en happy thou if so!
A million quick magnetic suns
'T would seem—yet 't is but One
That gives a ray to each on earth,
One bright sweet hope in life.
Some catch the ray and fondle it—
Ah, wise and happy they!
But there be others fear the world,

And dare not touch the Flame ;
Yet mourn in secret for its loss,
And so uncherished die.
For these, loved-mortals shed a tear,
And angels passing sigh.

THE EXISTENCE DUAL.

Visions of sleep! Their crowding forms
  On earth, in hell, in heaven move.
  Sleep doth not prove.
These are unreal—
Void fancies that we only feel.

There surely is some Life beyond
  The state of man's mere waking mind:
  Whereto—Earth-blind—
Men's spirits creep
From out the sepulchre of sleep.

Dream sleep—brief semblance of the
  " End "—

Wherein we die but for a night ;
Pass on to Light
Or down to hell
Oft—e'er the sexton toll the bell.

"THE LIGHTS OF NIGHT."

The lights of night who hath not seen?
The city lights, like fire-flies
Half-poised in air.   The river lights,
That dent and dimple as they go.
The lights of toil.   The lights of ease,
Where laughter rings.   The lights of
    death,
Where silence sits.   The curtained lights
Of love, that play with shadows on
A maiden's breast.   The watchman's light,
That moves awhile and then stands still.
The unexpected light, that stuns—
Revealing nothing but itself—
A flash! the centre of a blank,

As when hot lead hath slain a man.

The lights that dimly dwell o'er shrines.

The light that suddenly goes out,

As if the night had swallowed it,

And leaves us blind upon the road.

All these we know, as if we had

The trimming of the wicks.   The lights

Beyond us, are the living stars—

Undying in their mystery.

PARIS THE TON.

Yea, Paris, thou art France !
Fair senseless *ton*, my senses throb
For thee—thou art so beautiful.

Lord ! what a gad is Paris Fair,
Ripe bait for foreign hordes ;
You pay your chink and get your chunk
Well buttered on both sides.
The streets are watered every day,
The chestnut leaves are broad and green,
The opal absinthe's in the sunlit glass,
The fiacre-men curse each other as they go.
The "wide-eyed cities" of the Place
Concorde

Gaze on, and wonder when again
The grinning " Spectre" must come forth
Red-handed 'neath the quiet trees.
The ladies all step light as birds,
And some are pert and flip. There 're
    others
Not so fair—pale vampires with hairy lip
That sap the life of France—her bosom's
    foe.
Yea, Paris is a festive *ton*—a festive
Ton for all! Skate o'er on joy—
Thin crust of gilded, polished joy!
What matters it if Hell 's beneath?

"A LONELY STORK LOOKS DOWN THE RHINE."

A lonely Stork looks down the Rhine.

Behind, across the mead, four kingdoms
armed

Stand in their strength and flaunt their
flags.

The *pickelhaube* and the sway-back coat—

The goose-step and the folda-rol !

The fife and drum play English airs :

Yea, beer is better than absinthe.

The *mädchen* standing on the window-sill

Scrubs the imperfect glass with bare-armed

Energy.   Eight marks would keep her
for a month—

And yet her smile is generous.

Soap-suds are better than petroleum.

The good *Frau* knits in leisure time ;

But not upon a guillotine.

The old man in his cellar stews.

A child beneath a pillow lies.

A dog sleeps harnessed to a cart.

The sun shines broadly at mid-day

As *Herr Professor* stumbles forth—his
    eyes,

Gold-framed, bulge out above his beard.

The jagg'd-faced student doffs his cap,—
    and sings :

"A prince is better than a grocer's clerk."

Dann kommt acht bier und sechs cigarren
    —hi !

The goose-step and the folda-rol !

'T is night. The *Vaterland* 's at peace !

A WORD WITH AN OLD COMPANION.

How surely better now it would have been
Had I not made thee, pipe, my comfort-
er ;—
I 've grown dyspeptic in thy company !
And when I am most busy at my work
I needs must stop and ram thee with a
prod,—
Light countless matches at thy sweet ca-
price ;
Accursèd thing !—yet thou art dear to me.
Thou dost resemble me—so full of faults ;
Yet not so bad—when taking in account
How really wretched are most men and
things.

No ; I 'd not part with thee, though thou
    at times
Doth smell so rank (or so I have been
    told).
Perhaps I am unjust—it may be that
The strong tobacco that I feed thee with
Doth thee discredit in the eyes of men.
Howe'er this be, we 'll not discuss it more ;
Enough to say, thou art as dear to me
As guile must be to those who 'd slander
    thee.

NOLENS VOLENS.

Of all the wounds of life that cut deep
down
And mark the bone, there is a stubborn
sort
That gapes for aye—that festers in the
soul—
A hollow spectre in the memory,
Shrouded in folds of disappointment and
regret:
It is the void of wasted opportunities!
Why in great cities see we men so sad?
Hope should not break till life be snatched
And all best hopes fulfilled. "'T would
not

Be thus," say each apart, "had I
But spoken then, or acted when
The furnace blazed! Or e'en perchance
Breathed on the red-hot iron as it passed."
True what the poet saith, the saddest is :
    "*It might have been.*"
A gain may be maintained; but what is
    lost,
Is gone—forever lost! *Farewell for aye.*

THE EARTH'S ATHIRST.

Thou slanting rain! Thou Hebe of the
Skies,

That pours out drink to Earth; thou faith-
ful wife

That with moist tears embraces her prone
lord.

Thou mist intensified; thou double dew

That drowns the drought, that heals the
parched and burnt—

Thou resurrection rain. From thee comes
forth

New life—from water comes the ruby
blood—

The pulsing veins like thy blue streams,
O rain!

Thou liquid limpid rain, quick dust the
    leaves ;

Lay thy fresh cheek upon the heated
    grass ;

Soft kiss the rose and lift the lily's head,

Thou cooling muse, and like a fairy dance

Upon the beds. Come when the light-
    ning red

Hath struck and the tormented thunder
    groans,

In big round drops thou liquid limpid
    rain—

Come quickly then : say all is well, O rain !

THE DANCE OF LIFE.

Fate's certain wale bites in the cheek of
    hope,
Yet man persists to play the fool : 't is
    Life !
        Another to the Ball—
Time is the piper.   On the dance !
Were we but gods, concealed in some
Snug gallery, how we would laugh
To see poor mortals jump and writhe :
Th' expectant jaw, the tortured leg,
The haggard eyes—yet sanguine step—
In diverse jigs, in polk or waltz !
And over all, upon the air,
The jingle of discordant aims ;

It's music ceaseless—overpaid
In strife, and anguish, and despair
By each in some vain bootless quest . . .
Till all at once the lights go out !
Lo ! unexpectedly alone
We faint into the arms of Death—
The dark Recorder dips his pen :
      Another from the Ball.
Experience, History, Fathers—sing :
Each cradled kid doth pule but for his
    fling !

THROUGH A GLASS DARKLY.

This is a very little world ;
And the people round about us,
We meet and meet again.   Till almost
Like a prison it would seem ;
With stated limits, where beyond
We could not pass, in fear of meeting
There without, an unfamiliar face ;
Some being, that somewhere we had not
In our waking or in dreaming seen before.
Yet can we be the only species
That exists above the brute creation ?
Were it not vain to rest so satisfied—
Contented with the mere reflection
In our eyes, as 't were a neighbor's mirror—

Each man a faulty copy of the next?
And is there not a craving in the heart
For grander, nobler, fairer forms
Than daily meet our view.   A longing—
Here perhaps, imperfectly. expressed—
To see, if but for once, the Face of God?

DIES NON.

Away to the river—or glittering sand ;
  We 'll cast our cares on the stream,
We 'll watch them float past to the ends
    of the land,
  While we sit passive and dream.

Or to the wide ocean—in ships to the sea—
  And rest our cares on the shore ;
We 'll lie on the crest that is idle and free,
  Nor look to the land any more.

We 'll speed to the mountains—or high
    on the hills—
  And leave our troubles below ;
Draw near unto heaven, that o'er all our ills
  The waters of *nihil* may flow.

THE SPIRIT ON THE WALL.

I.

Death in death is naught,
But death in life is all—
For dying then we die indeed :
Our evil spirits walk abroad,
While all that 's good within us sleeps.

I have a picture* in my room,
A portrait hanging on the wall.
It shows a quiet woman's face,
Shrouded in black, with folds that fall
Beneath the heavy frame.   A modern
Magdalen, 't is thought. It has a jewelled

* The original in the Dresden Gallery, by Jean Libert Oury.

Cross upon its breast—an open book be-
    fore.
The cross is jewelled, mark—and the still
    face,
Repentant though 't would seem to be—
The eyes did surely sin again.
One winter's night, 't was snowing fast,
Perchance else this, my steps were heard—
I sudden came, and quickly entered in.
When, lo ! on glancing up, the face had
    gone—
The frame hung empty o'er my head !
And yet the wicked eyes burnt in my soul
From out the centre of the void, as if
They still were there !   Chilled, and half-
    dazed,
I seized a sword (the first thing that I
    saw)—

And light before, I wheeled about :
A noiseless shadow flashed me past !
She had gone back !   I was too late !
I sprang and tore her from the wall,
Or what I madly thought had life—
Life of some sort, unknown to me :—
Nothing, nothing ! The canvas as before.

II.

Although I curse thee every night ;
Yet let thy image still be on my wall—
'T were better there than in my heart.
Had Cain a wife, she were like thee !
Why such reproach in thy fixed eyes ?
The Human brood is one.   Yea, I 'm like
 thee !
The power to do good, the willingness to
 sin,

Are both within us pent.   The war goes
   on—
The battle in the Soul.   Perchance 't is
   fiercer
In thy breast.   And this would mark thee
   out
More Human than the rest— thus more
Deserving of a gentler sympathy.
Forget, if I were harsh awhile,
And let me turn to thee again,
And crave forgiveness in a look.—
Yet stay ?   The Devil 's in those eyes—
No, no !   I cannot say : *Amen !*

THE BECKONING DEPTHS.

The writhing eddies in the night,
   Like curving serpents on the sand,
   Caress with their smooth sides the land,
Disporting in the moon's dead light.

What lieth 'neath these cone-shaped
     moils ?
   Some naiad girl may gaze above
   Upon the stars, and dream of love
From the deep apex of their coils ;

May long to be a child of earth,
   May yearn for human love divine :
   For some terrestrial troth may pine,
And mourn her water-wasted birth ;

Curse the slow drifting walls of wave
   While she untangles her long hair ;
   With cold chaste hope awaiting there
Some brave to wed her in her grave.

I 'm but a desperate man !   Here, wrong
   Or right, to-night, beneath this tide,
   I 'll make this forlorn maid my bride :
Die ! as the swan that ends his song.

HEART OF GRACE.

Mourn not ! rejected, faint, unheeded
    bard,
  If thou but be a Poet true,
Thy day must come ! Though yet the
    way is hard
  As ever 't was with those that sue.

Faith in thy Muse alone sustain thee
    while
Oblivious fame is still asleep.
At any time she may awake and smile ;
  What folly then for thee to weep !

Sing on, sing on ! The numbers of thy
    songs,
If not thy voice must wake her soon ;
Then will it be her turn to mourn the
    wrongs
Done to the lark, that sings at noon !

"WHAT 'S IN A NAME ?"

Can justice with compassion mate ?
Can strength with pity play ? Say, friend,
'T is as thou wilt : Wouldst thou prefer
The semblance to the thing ?   Or else
The *thing*—with " semblance " to the
  dogs?
This is the question of all politics.
Though " Liberty " is but a name ; yet
Should it mean what 's real, and really
  dear,
In its integrity unto the hearts of men.

THE GAME OF CHESS.

I.

This chess-board is the even grassy lawn
For dress parade.   A soldier is a pawn ;
A knight is cavalry—a boomerang thing.
The Queen is keeper of an infirm King,
A monarch strangely subject to a scare.
The sidelong bishops flank the royal pair.
And out upon the checkered border-land
Two watchful towers at the corner stand.
Between these stretch the soldier-pawns in
    field,
In line of battle like a moving shield.

II.

The sides are drawn and White begins to
    play,

Then quickly Black comes out and stops
the way.

Now a White venturous knight attacks
the Black ;

A bishop comes, the knight goes slowly
back ;

A castle moves, the Queen comes now in
aid ;

The Blacks (that should not venture)
make a raid.

The White King menaced, *castles* in a
fright,—

Yet now 't is changed—I am attacked by
White.

III.

Now comes the fray, the battle of the mind,

Down bent upon the board some plot to
bind ;

To look into the fabricked web of thought,

Discern the vantage point that must be
    caught,

And from it build the structure of a *mate;*

Find some weak fissure, and there storm
    the gate.

Now here comes White again, but this is
    vain—

Why that queer move ? there 's nothing
    there to gain.

I 'm sure this player 's overrated.

What ! can it be ? but I 'm *checkmated !*

"OF TIME."

Time is the noiceless axis of the Earth.

The track on which our bodies run,

Our hearts are different ; some souls

Go on with life's Earth engine mate ;

But others, like the smoke that living
makes

In a high spirit wind, are blown before.

Yet these are few, while as 't is said,

The greater number fall behind their
earthly

Semblance in the flesh, and leave a grimy

Wake that for an instant marks their
course—

Forgotten when the morrow brings the
rain.

The first short span is Human Life,
Until we reach the cross-roads—Death.
How ribald Time doth fool us in his
    sleeve :
Fan the fair bloom from Beauty's cheek,
    then laugh
To see the wreck : A raddled Harridan,
Who still smiles at her glass—the last to
    credit
The stale fact. How Time doth lash us
    with sharp pains,
Set loose our teeth, snatch wisps of hair,
    dim eyes—
And finally bend our backs toward earth
To find the fittest place for burial.

Time is a wandering Jew, that cannot
Pause to rest ; and yet bestrides
Us with his various usuries.

Time is the refuge of the old man's brain
In all the sweet still joys of memory,
When action stores no more the chamber
Of events, and space is covered up.

Time heals or cuts again.   Time's hair-
    spring probes
Into the secret treasure of events ;
As the lost Past was solved, so must
The Future riddle-out what 's *now.*
'T is patience only that can crane
The slipp'ry neck of Time ; and steal
A purchase in some deadly hope.

Time is the publisher of facts
And loveth downright truth.   He doth
Proclaim the good, expose the bad,
Without discussion or make-shift—
And sets us all to wondering !